A Mexican Wedding Celebration

La Boda

by
Nancy Van Laan

Illustrated by
Andrea Arroyo

Little, Brown and Company
Boston   New York   Toronto   London

Glossary

Abuela (ah-BWAY-lah) . . . . — Grandmother

la boda (lah BOH-dah) . . . . — the wedding

los barrenderos (lohs bah-ren-DAY-rohs) . . . . — the sweepers

la bendición (lah ben-dee-SYOHN) . . . . . . — the blessing

caramelitos (kah-rah-may-LEE-tohs) . . . . — little candies

la casa de la boda (lah KAH-sah day lah BOH-dah) . — the house of the wedding

los cuetes (lohs CWAY-tays) . . . . — the fireworks

higadito (ee-gah-DEE-toh) . . . . — a mixture of egg, meat, and spices

la iglesia (lah ee-GLAY-zee-ah) . . . . . . — the church

jarabe (hah-RAH-bay) . . . . — dance music

mole (MOH-lay) . . . . — a meat dish with chili and chocolate

los músicos (lohs MOO-zee-kohs) . . . . . . — the musicians

el palomo (el pah-LOH-moh) . . . . — the dove

los pavos (lohs PAH-vohs) . . . . — the turkeys

por siempre (pohr SYEM-pray) . . . . . . — forever

la procesión (lah proh-say-SYOHN) . . . . . — the procession

rosario (roh-SAH-ree-oh) . . . . — flower necklace

los tíos (lohs TEE-ohs) . . . . — the uncles

tortillas (tor-TEE-yahs) . . . . — flat corn bread

To Enrique — *gracias!*
— N. V. L.

For Felipe Galindo, *con amor*
— A. A.

Text copyright © 1996 by Nancy Van Laan
Illustrations copyright © 1996 by Andrea Arroyo

First Edition

Calligraphy by Mary Anne Lloyd

Library of Congress Cataloging-in-Publication Data

Van Laan, Nancy.
  La boda : a Mexican wedding celebration / by Nancy Van Laan ;
  illustrated by Andrea Arroyo. — 1st ed.
    p. cm.
  Text primarily in English with some Spanish.
  Summary: A little girl and her grandmother watch as the whole village prepares for and participates in a traditional Zapotec Indian wedding celebration.
  ISBN 0-316-89626-8
  [1. Zapotec Indians — Social life and customs — Fiction. 2. Indians of Mexico — Social life and customs — Fiction. 3. Weddings — Fiction.]
  I. Arroyo, Andrea, ill. II. Title.
  PZ7.V3269Bo   1996
  [E] — dc20   94-39169

10 9 8 7 6 5 4 3 2 1

NIL

Published simultaneously in Canada by Little, Brown & Company (Canada) Limited and in Great Britain by Little, Brown and Company (UK) Limited

Printed in Italy

The paintings for this book were done in watercolor and ink on Arches watercolor paper.

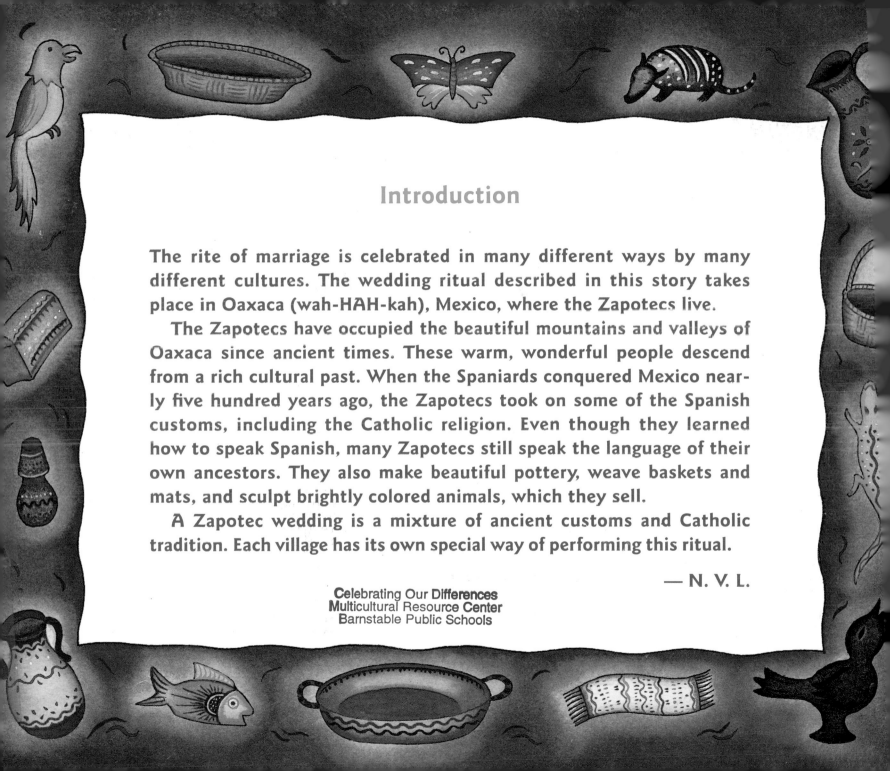

Introduction

The rite of marriage is celebrated in many different ways by many different cultures. The wedding ritual described in this story takes place in Oaxaca (wah-HAH-kah), Mexico, where the Zapotecs live.

The Zapotecs have occupied the beautiful mountains and valleys of Oaxaca since ancient times. These warm, wonderful people descend from a rich cultural past. When the Spaniards conquered Mexico nearly five hundred years ago, the Zapotecs took on some of the Spanish customs, including the Catholic religion. Even though they learned how to speak Spanish, many Zapotecs still speak the language of their own ancestors. They also make beautiful pottery, weave baskets and mats, and sculpt brightly colored animals, which they sell.

A Zapotec wedding is a mixture of ancient customs and Catholic tradition. Each village has its own special way of performing this ritual.

— N. V. L.

Today is *la boda.*
The what, Abuela?
La boda, Maria.
Today is *the wedding* of Alfonso
   and Luisa.

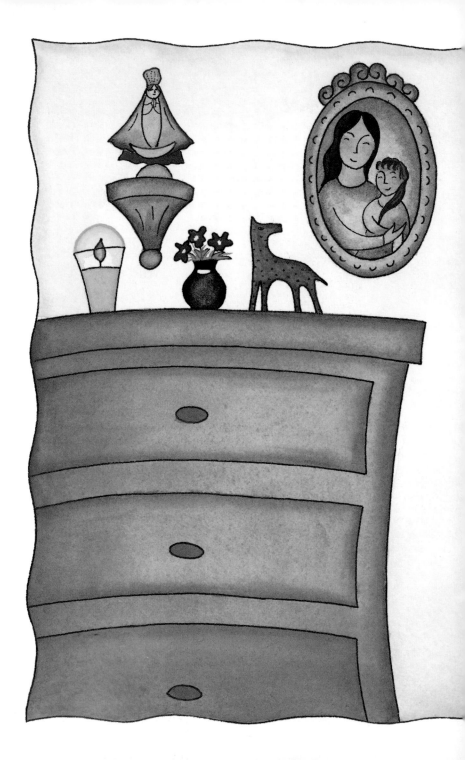

Those are *los barrenderos.*
The who, Abuela?
Los barrenderos, Maria.
The sweepers are cleaning
la casa de la boda.
They are sweeping the streets
and *the house of the wedding.*

Here come *los músicos.*
The who?
Los músicos.
Those are *the musicians* who
  play for *la boda.*

And here come *los tíos.*
The *uncles*, Abuela?
Yes, the uncles, Maria.
These three uncles announce
la boda.

Off go *los tíos*.
Off go *los músicos*.
Is it time for *la boda*?
Yes, it is time for *la boda*.
It is time for the wedding
    of Alfonso and Luisa.

Here comes Alfonso,
his father and mother.
And his sisters and brothers?
Yes — and some others.

Next comes Luisa,
her family and guests.
Then it is our turn.
Am I a guest?
Yes!

Now we must follow.
We follow each other?
Yes, we follow each other,
one after the other,
to gather together
at *la iglesia.*
The what?
La iglesia.
The church
in the square.

Shhh! Alfonso and Luisa
are saying their vows.
"...*por siempre,*" says Luisa.
"...*por siempre,*" says Alfonso.
They promise to stay
together *forever.*

Boom!

What's that, Abuela?
Los cuetes, Maria.
The fireworks go off for Alfonso
  and Luisa!

Does the band play?
Yes, it plays all the way
to *la casa de la boda.*
The house that is covered
with flowers from the
  mountains?
Yes, *la casa de la boda,*
where we shall all eat.

Mole, higadito, and tortillas
we eat:
chili mixed with chocolate;
eggs, spices, meat.

Look! Alfonso feeds his
   godmother,
and she feeds Alfonso.
Luisa feeds her godfather,
and he feeds Luisa.

Now the band plays *jarabe,*
music for dancing.
They play "El Palomo,"
the dance called "The Dove."

As we hear fireworks
and listen to *jarabe,*
we say, "Alfonso and Luisa
are eating like doves."

Like chili and chocolate,
we all mix together.
Yes! And the sky like a sunrise
brightens with fireworks!
Come, let us follow
the newlyweds home.

Are Alfonso and Luisa
now husband and wife?
Yes! May they always be happy.
May they live a long life!

Out in the streets now,
everyone is dancing!
I love to dance!
I love to dance, too.

And here's your *rosario*,
pretty *flowers* to wear.

Get ready for *caramelitos!*
Little candies, Abuela?
Yes, and bags of confetti
and good things to eat.

Now for *la bendición*.
The blessing, Abuela?
Yes, everyone gives a blessing.
Everything is blessed.

It's time for *la procesión*!
The what, Abuela?
The procession, Maria.
It's time for the parade
of gifts for the bride.
Oh, good, Abuela!
Now I can bring mine.

It is time for *los pavos*.
The what, Abuela?
The turkeys, Maria.
The dance of the turkeys
is such fun to see!

Look, Abuela —
the turkeys are dancing!
The men hold their wings
and dance along, too!

Van Laan, Nancy

La boda

$15.45

DATE			